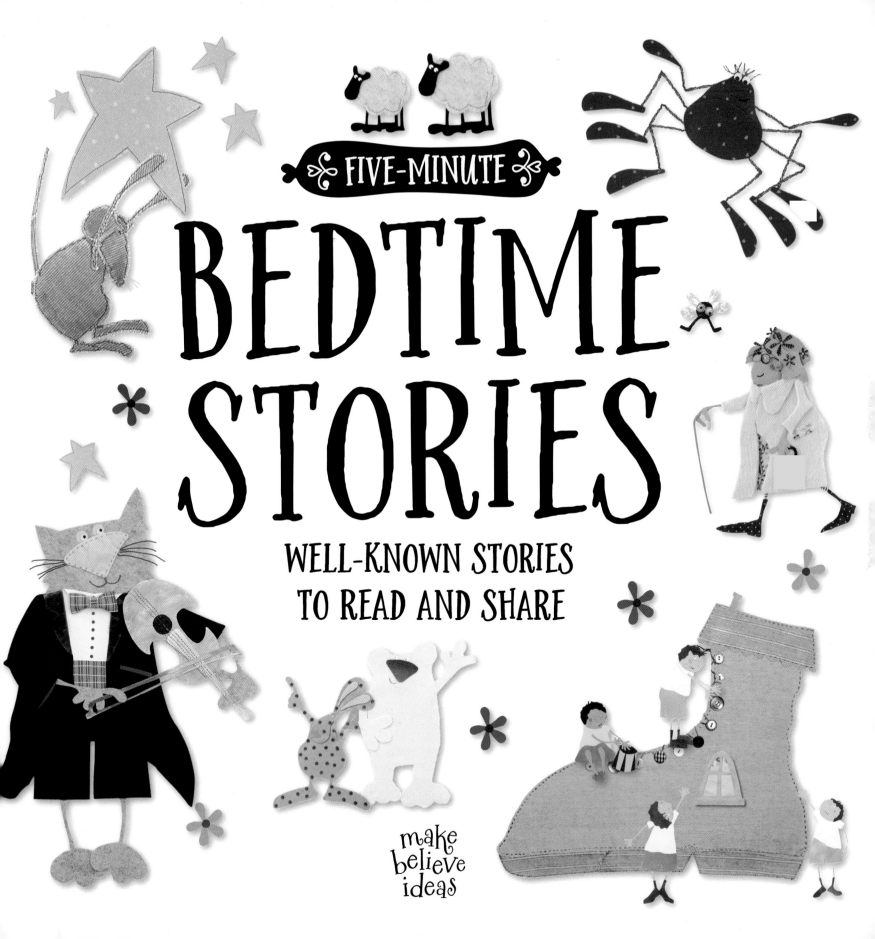

FIVE-MINUTE

BEDTIME STORIES

WELL-KNOWN STORIES TO READ AND SHARE

make
believe
ideas

ILLUSTRATED BY KATE TOMS

 CONTENTS

TWINKLE TWINKLE LITTLE STAR

Twinkle, twinkle, little star, how I wonder what you are.

You shine above the world so high, like a lightbulb in the sky.

Twinkle, twinkle, little **star**,
I do so **wonder** what **you** are.

When **snuggled** up in **bed** at night,

cozy, **warm**, and **tucked** up tight,

5

I dream that I can fly a rocket . . .

5 4 3 2

and gather stardust in my pocket.

1

Blast off!

7

Twinkle, twinkle, little star,
what do **you** see from afar?

Hello!

¡Hola!

8

Are there **mice** just like me
living way across the **sea?**

Guten Tag!

Bonjour!

Ciao!

9

Are there **stars** for us **all** up there?

All mine!

Wheeeeee!

Jump!

Or do some folks have to share?

11

Twinkle, twinkle, little **star**, how I wonder what **you** are!

Wheeeeeeeee!

I want to be a **star** like you,

and see the **world** the way you do.

Twinkle, twinkle, little star,
how I wonder what you are.

When it's time to climb the stairs,

to **brush** my **teeth**
and say my **prayers**,

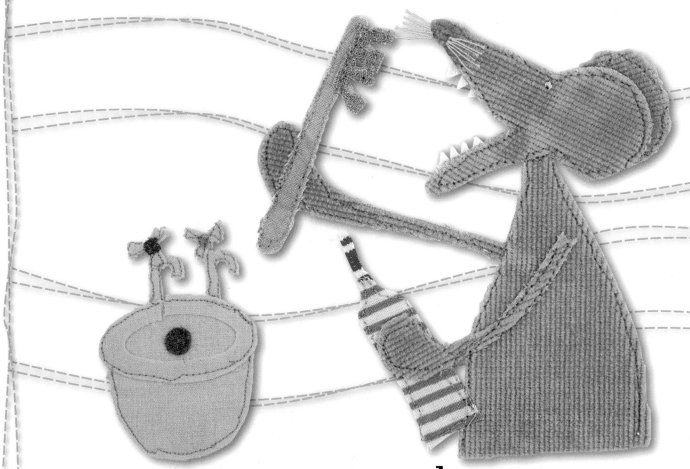

through my **window** I can see
that you are **smiling** down on me.

Twinkle, twinkle, little star,
how I wonder what you are.

There's **so** much **more** I'd like to **say**, maybe we'll **talk** **another** day.

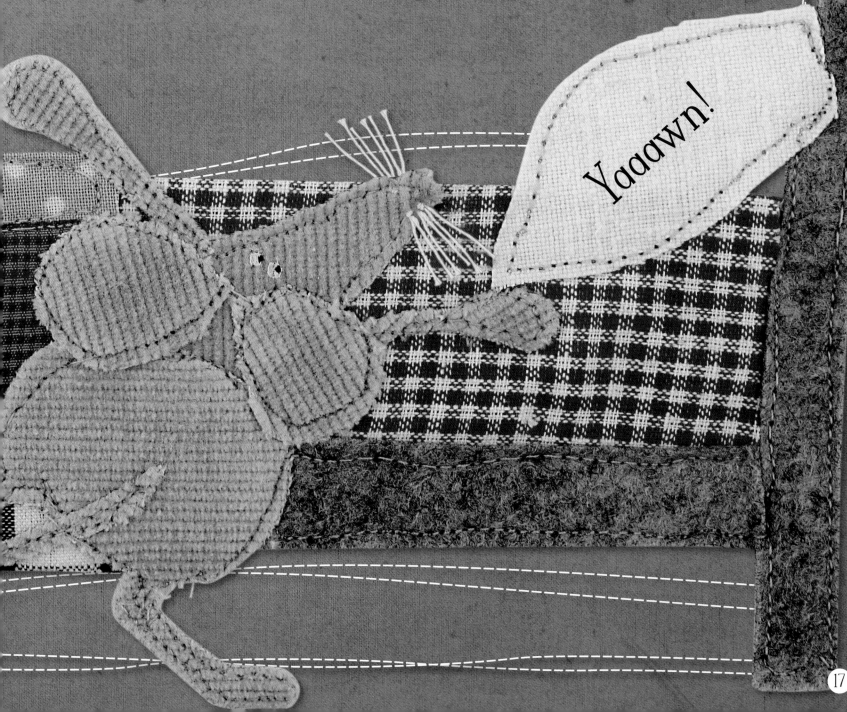

INCY WINCY SPIDER

Incy Wincy Spider
went UP the water spout.

Down came the rain,
and washed the spider OUT.

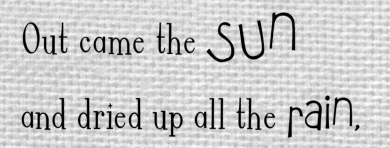

Out came the SUN

and dried up all the rain,

so Incy Wincy Spider

climbed up the spout again.

Here we go again!

19

But why does INCY climb the SpOut?

(In case you are in any doubt.)

Because he's SPUN his web up high,

so he can See the world go by . . .

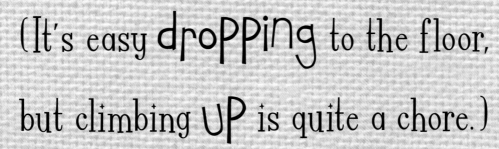

(It's easy **dropping** to the floor,

but climbing **UP** is quite a chore.)

21

Incy Wincy Spider

doesn't like the rain,

he's got his swimming goggles on,

(he won't get caught again).

But . . . just as he starts climbing UP the water spout, another shower of rain falls down

and washes Incy out!

Uh-oh!

Now **Incy's** trying once again,
umbrella **at the ready**.
The **rain** won't beat him **this** time
if he takes it
nice and **steady**.

There has to be another way

to get home on a rainy day!

Looking **around**, what's **INCY** seen?
A **round** and **bouncy** trampoline!

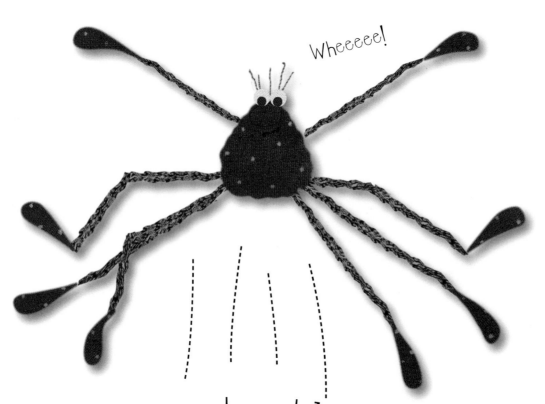

Wheeeee!

He's found a way to get home fast . . .

but bounces high

and flies straight past...

Not again!

Over the hedge,
over the wall,

a stripy tent

breaks his fall.

Looking puzzled,
Incy thinks.

He rubs his hairy head and blinks.

27

The **washing's** out,

the **weather's** fine,

Incy wobbles on the line,

when suddenly a breezy breeze blows Incy to some nearby trees.

Through the leaves, **Incy** spies several pairs of **beady eyes.**

"But **worse** than that," **Incy** squeaks, "a row of **long** and **pointy** beaks."

Aaaaargh!

INCY'S running, quite PuFFed out,

but in the distance,

sees the SPOUT.

It's the **best** idea
he's had **all day**.
He'll climb the spout
another way.

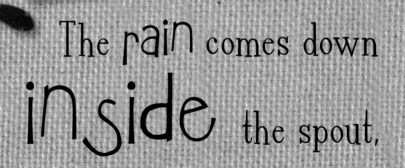

The **rain** comes down
inside the spout,

so he'll climb **UP**

not in, but out!

Back in his **web**,

he's **happy** now.

(It's easy when you've worked out how . . .)

The lesson **learned?**

Try, try again . . . .

and don't be put off by the rain!

Home at last!

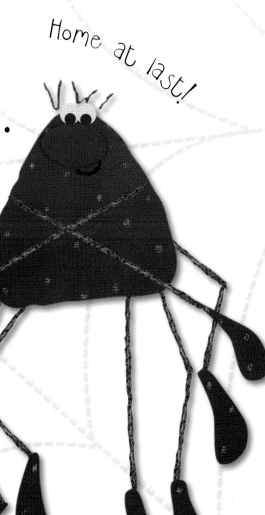

So **Incy Wincy Spider**
can **climb** the water spout.
And even if the **rain pours down**,
it can't wash **Incy** out.

For **Incy Wincy Spider**

has found **another** way,

and now it's "**easy-peasy**"

UP I go!

to climb the spout **all day.**

THE OLD
WOMAN
WHO LIVED
IN A SHOE

There was an **old woman** who lived in a shoe,

with so many **children** —

what could they all do?

Every day, they'd have some fun,

but not until

the **chores** were done!

On **Monday,** they have clothes to wash,
and sheets to **clean**
with a **splish** and a **splosh.**

Spinning around in the **big** machine, the washing is soon all fresh and clean.

soapso

On **Tuesday,** every child must choose
some polish and a pair of shoes.

They **scrape** and **brush** and **polish** hard,
in a line out in the yard.

shoe Polish

shoe Polish

Later on, they go for a **swim,**
put armbands on and **JUMP** right in!

They **laugh** and **dive**
and **splash about**

and towels are **ready**
when they get out.

On **Wednesday,** they get on their knees
to pick some **carrots, beans** and **peas** —
there's lots of **digging,** gathering **berries**
and filling bowls with piles of **cherries!**
Then . . .

It's **music time** for girls and boys,

lots of **singing**, lots of **noise!**

They **dance** and **sing** and **twirl** around

and make a really **lovely** sound.

On **Thursday,** a trip to the vet's

to get a **check-up** for the **pets.**

Once they are **home,** they brush the **fur.**

Listen to the kittens **purrr!**

On **Friday,** it's off to the **park** to play —
a **happy** way to spend the day.

A **picnic's** packed, the buggy's full —
and don't forget the **bouncy** ball!

By **Saturday,** the cupboard's **bare.**
The **old woman** sits in her **chair**

to write a **list** of things they need,
with so many **hungry** mouths to **feed!**

A **shopping** trip
is quickly planned,
and everybody
lends a hand.

48

Soon the **trolley's**
piled up high
with all the things
they need to **buy.**

49

Sunday is the day of rest –
see them in their
Sunday best,

all in a row, **one** by **one**.
Can you **remember**
the **things** they've done?

Hey diddle diddle,
the cat and the fiddle,

the cow

jumps over

the Moon,

the little dog laughs
to see
such fun,

and the dish runs away with the spoon.

Hey diddle diddle, when Cat plays his fiddle, Dog sings along to the tune,

Cow's in the bath,

then Dog starts to **laugh**
when Dish **comes back**
with the **spoon.**

The piggies all prance,

the elephants dance,

and, hand in hand,
the kangaroos stand,

tapping their toes to the tune!

Hey diddle diddle,
Cat hangs up his fiddle
and Moon looks down from on high.

and everyone's waving bye-bye.

THE OLD LADY WHO SWALLOWED A FLY

There was an **old lady** who **swallowed** a fly.

Why, oh **why,** did she swallow a **fly?**

Oh my, oh my!

Tra la la!

That little old lady
was **walking** along,
enjoying the sunshine
and **singing** a song.
When **all of a sudden**

a fly flew south,

and ended up flying right into her **mouth!**
That **poor** old lady – what a to-do!
Imagine if that happened to **you!**

The fly now buzzes and **tickles** her **tummy**
(she didn't think it tasted so yummy)!

But **suddenly** she has an **idea**

to make the naughty fly disappear:

to catch the fly she swallows

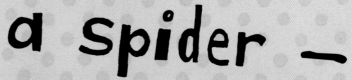

a spider —

so now she has them **both** inside her!

Oh my, oh my!

Down by the pond she **spots** a **frog**, sitting still on a speckled log.

Without even saying, "How do you do?"

cRoAK! she picks up the frog and **swallows** him too!

Feeling just a **little** queasy

(certainly not so bright and breezy),

she **spots** a heron on a nest –

I wonder if **you** can

guess the rest?

How **absurd** . . .
to swallow a **bird**!

Oh my, oh my!

How could she **do** that?
We don't know how —
but you won't **believe**

what happens now . . . .

Pretty Kitty sits and **purrs**;
from behind her something **stirs.**

Before **poor puss**
has time
to flee . . .

cREaM

By this time it's **getting dark.**
Prince the **dog** plays in the park.

But poor old Prince
just does not see
the **old lady**
lurking by a big tree.

GULP!

Poor Prince . . .

The old lady's **tummy** is fit to **burst** – she wishes she'd thought more **carefully** first.

She swallowed the **dog**
to catch the cat.
She swallowed the **cat**
to catch the bird.
She swallowed the **bird**
to catch the frog.
She swallowed the **frog**
to catch the spider.
She swallowed the **spider**
to catch the fly . . .

if **only** that fly had just **flown by.**

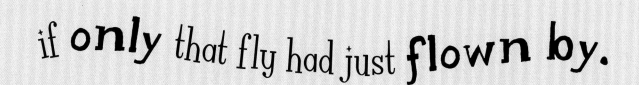
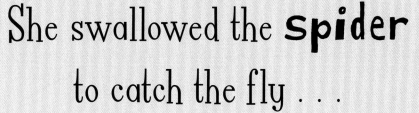

I UDDERLY LOVE YOU

Udderley
sque-e-eze!
I love
everything about you:
your tail, your ears,
your toes.

I love the softness of your skin, your silky, s-moo-th, wet nose.

83

I love your every **moo**-vement,

the way you skip about,

and how your

hooves

point inwards,

while all your **knees** stick out!

I love the way
you chatter,
the funny things you say,
the **moo**-sic
that you sing to me,

And when you go exploring, it makes me really proud,

tweet! tweet!

Grrr! Grrr!

DOG

to know you'll always find me,

MOO! MOO! MOO! MOO! MOO!

MOO!

MOO!

even in a crowd.

At night-time, in the
moo-nlight,
when the stars shine overhead,

I watch you as you're sleeping
in your snuggly, little bed.

I love you when you're happy.

ha-ha!
ha-ha!

I love you when you're sad.

moo-hoo!

Even when you're **moo**-dy,
not meaning to be bad.

NO! NO!
NO!

Every day with you is special,
I love you
through and through,

I UDDERLY, UDDERLY LOVE YOU

and I know you love me too!

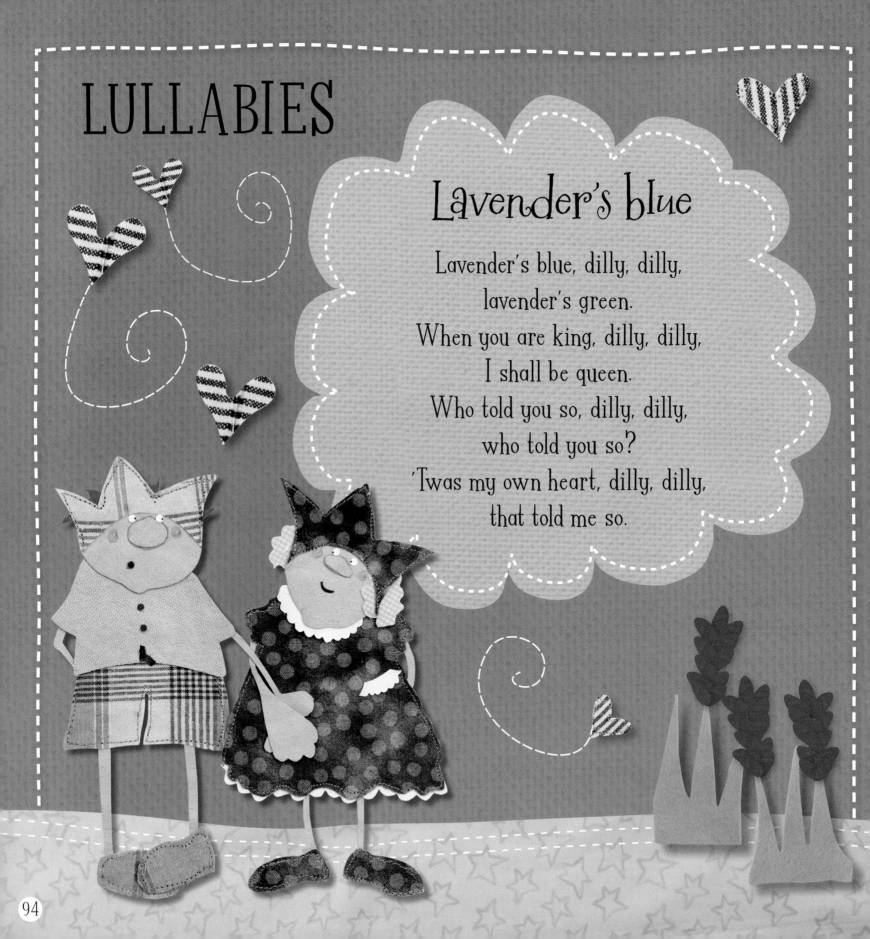

LULLABIES

Lavender's blue

Lavender's blue, dilly, dilly,
lavender's green.
When you are king, dilly, dilly,
I shall be queen.
Who told you so, dilly, dilly,
who told you so?
'Twas my own heart, dilly, dilly,
that told me so.

Sleep, Baby, sleep

Sleep, Baby, sleep,
long and safe and deep.
The wind will blow
the dreamland tree
and from it shake
sweet dreams for thee.
Sleep, Baby, sleep,
our cottage vale is deep.
The little lamb
is on the green,
with snowy fleece
so soft and clean.
Sleep, Baby, sleep.

Rock-a-bye, Baby

Rock-a-bye, Baby,
on the treetop.
When the wind blows,
the cradle will rock.
When the bough breaks,
the cradle will fall,
and down will come Baby,
cradle and all.